JOHN'S EYES

JOANNA CORRANCE

LUNA NOVELLA #1

Text Copyright © 2021 Joanna Corrance
Cover © 2021 Jay Johnstone

First published by Luna Press Publishing, Edinburgh, 2021

John's Eyes ©2021. All rights reserved. No part of this publication may be reproduced, stored in a retrieval system, or transmitted in any form or by any means, electronic, mechanical, photocopy, recording or oth- erwise, without prior written permission of the copyright owners. Nor can it be circulated in any form of binding or cover other than that in which it is published and without similar condition including this condition being imposed on a subsequent purchaser.

www.lunapresspublishing.com
ISBN-13: 978-1-913387-43-3.

For Tom, with love

Contents

Chapter One

The day I met John was at the clinic during our initial consultation to ensure we were compatible. He was everything I had hoped he would be. Where I was new and glossy, John was dishevelled and broken. His untidy facial hair was a contrast to the smooth faces of the male doctors who fussed over us. Doctors were easy to recognise because they were robed in white and serious behind glistening smiles. Doctors made John nervous, but I didn't mind them. They were always gentle with me.

They let John feel me as they talked him through the process. The tone of his voice was different to the clinical staff; I came to understand that tone as nervousness. Whilst my primary function was to give John sight, I was also programmed to monitor his emotions. That way I would be able to filter his vision appropriately. Initially I felt overwhelmed by his data, rushing to interpret what he meant by the beat of his heart and the signals from his brain. The doctors were certain that it wouldn't take me long to become fluent. They said that I was intelligent.

John had been blind for seven years. He explained to the

doctor at the consultation that it was down to degenerative change – '*nothing dramatic*' he had said with a hint of bitterness to his tone. I noticed the clinician drop her smile as he said it, deeming the practiced smile inappropriate. I found this peculiar, given she knew that he couldn't see her.

Chapter Two

John was devastated when they removed his eyes. It puzzled me at first because they were broken and deemed unfixable. They needed to be thrown away, just as I would happily be if I failed to serve my purpose. Yet John wept for his faulty organic matter. When they synced us up at the clinic and I began to understand John better, I realised that he wept because it had meant there was no hope of him achieving natural sight ever again. When he thought of his first eyes, his heart beat a little faster and I could sense his sadness. It felt like falling heavily without ever landing. His first eyes had been the colour of milky coffee and people had always said they were friendly eyes. I, however, was pale blue in appearance. John joked with the nurses that he looked like a vampire. Although he parroted their chuckling, I could tell that he wasn't really laughing. I felt the falling sensation as he quietly mourned those useless brown orbs.

We spent our first few days together in the rehabilitation centre, where John's clumsy movements were closely monitored. I set about measuring and resizing images so that, eventually, John could assess distance. I also altered the filters so that the world appeared in colours that pleased him. Soon, John was walking without stumbling and his heart thumped steadily in his chest, which had inflated with joy. I was rewarded with ticks on a clipboard as the nurses nodded in approval. I swelled with pride.

When the doctors asked John if he was happy with me, he replied with 'I love them'.

Love.

Chapter Three

I had never seen the world outside the clinic before. My birthplace was a steel room filled with tubes and machines that bleeped and flashed. The doctor's consultation rooms, the theatre and the recovery rooms were built in the same style. Grey and white with flashing green and red lights. Green was good and red was bad. That seemed to be a set rule, which was strange, because one day a doctor's husband came in and surprised her with red flowers which were an even more vicious crimson than the red lights. She seemed delighted. Perhaps it meant that red wasn't always bad. I was going to have to work hard to understand the subtleties of these meanings.

John and I left the clinic together. They offered him a complimentary taxi, but he chose to walk, excited by the prospect of seeing the world around him for the first time in seven years. I worked fast, dabbling with the colours and brightness of the streets and buildings. It was a challenge compared to the stark whites and blues of the clinic. I sensed John's heartbeat increase, but in a different way; instead of falling it felt like he was floating. His complex matter exploded with endorphins. I logged the subtlety of it.

Initially, I was startled by the colourful machinery that hurtled towards John at a speed that would harm, if not end, his life. Interestingly, he wasn't afraid and simply continued to stroll ahead on the black tarmac as they whipped passed him. I began to understand that there were rules that the moving machines were obliged to follow. John was safe so long as he was aware of those rules. The lights on the road flashed red and he stopped. Green meant go. Red was bad and green was good. However, I glanced at the people inside the moving machines and wondered what the colours meant to them. At the clinic, John had asked about the moving machines that he referred to as cars and was informed he would not be allowed to drive one until the completion of our trial period. I found myself relieved; it was too early for me to take on such responsibility.

I was surprised to see that there was nobody else like me outside. At the clinic I had often rolled over to observe my friends, either tucked neatly in their glass cases or, for the lucky ones, filling the sockets of their people. Out on the streets, I felt suddenly alone. The fleshy orbs fixed into the people who walked by us either ignored us entirely or, when they did look, looked through me, seeing only John. Nevertheless, that was unimportant. I had a job to do. As much as I would have liked my friends to come with me, my work had to take priority.

We arrived at the train station and at our stop, we walked for nearly an hour before reaching John's home. He lived in a block of bricks with lots of other people who all owned sections of the building. Inside some of the sections, there were multiple people. Some of the people were very little with plump faces and a clumsy gait. The little people were accompanied by larger people. I was relieved to find that John had no little people in his section; I struggled to interpret their noises. They shrieked and yet their faces wore an expression I had to learnt to mean happiness. Peculiar.

Flat. John called it 'a flat'. It was another one of the words that had multiple meanings. Contrary to my understanding of its definition, John's flat was anything but. The ceilings were high and corniced with extravagant designs. I was displeased by the irregularity of the edges in the flat. None of them were as neat as back in the clinic.

I could tell that John was disappointed by what he saw. He considered his surroundings bland and scrunched up his face in distaste at the bars that surrounded the walls and the red buttons with red cords that hung from the ceiling. I was uncertain if they were the good red or the bad red. Going by John's reaction to them, I had to assume that they were bad. He walked slowly towards a cupboard, holding his breath as he opened it. There was a small wooden block on the floor with a coiled metal design and a small, mould covered piece of food perched delicately on a metal end. I analysed its components and identified it as a trap. Fortunately, it was too small to cause John any harm. He sighed in relief and shut the cupboard door.

Examining his reflection in the bathroom mirror, John ran his index finger down the groove of his cheekbone and stroked the line of his jaw, admiring how different he looked when he was clean-shaven. I recalled how he had told a nurse that he was nervous about seeing himself for the first time in seven years, uncertain as to whether he had aged well.

Therefore, I adjusted the filter so that the lines beside me smoothed out and the flecks of grey in his head of curls were seen to be the colour of toffee. He smiled with satisfaction at his reflection, revealing teeth that appeared straighter to him. Proud, I fantasised about the tick on the clipboard. I missed the direct praise that I had become accustomed to at the clinic, but was aware that I would now have to derive satisfaction from my successes. I awarded myself a tick on an imaginary clipboard.

Chapter Four

I noticed an interesting sensation when John looked at the woman who lived in the flat opposite him on the ground floor of our tenement. His heartbeat increased, as it often did at sudden changes in his environment, but his groin became simultaneously hot and tense. I interpreted it as being both pleasing and frustrating for John.

Her name was Francine and she had lived in the building for two years. She had always been kind to John, taking his arm at the step by the tenement entrance or offering to pick up the occasional necessity from the shop for him. She worked as a sales assistant at a nearby bookshop to pay her bills but preferred to describe her occupation as 'artist'. I knew this because he talked to his parents about her on the telephone. His father told John that he should ask her out, while his mother muttered in the distance not to encourage him.

"John!" Francine exclaimed when she first saw him coming out of his flat. "How did it go – the surgery?" She bent down and stared at me curiously. To my pleasure, she was staring at *me*, not John. Francine looked at me for what I was, not just an extension of John. "They're beautiful."

I liked her immediately.

She wore a small gold stud in her delicate nose and her hair was the colour of rusty penny coins. John and I both marvelled at her colouring. I could tell John wanted to reach out and touch her rouged cheek. His hand twitched by his side.

With a flicker of excitement, I realised I could help John. One morning, when he was taking the bins out, I heard her voice on the stairwell before we opened the door. I quickly adjusted the filter so that when John opened the door, he saw her standing before him completely naked. She was on the phone but mouthed '*good morning*' to him with a friendly wave before resuming her conversation. John paused, staring at her in surprise. Her white flesh was smooth and creamy, upper thighs and hips pleasantly fleshy. I evened out her breasts and reduced them slightly so that they sat pert against her chest without the need for support. I had seen images on John's computer screen before, so I knew what would please him. John realised he was staring and muttered a flustered good morning. Francine looked bemused as he passed. When he met his friends at a place he called 'the pub', he recanted the event in excitable tones.

"*Totally* naked?" John's friend David raised a heavy black eyebrow in disbelief. They sat around a table in a noisy and dimly lit space. I was forced to increase the brightness so that John could better make out his friends' faces and the surrounds. On realising how grimy it was and how this displeased John, I lowered it back down a little more than I would have liked to ensure that John continued to enjoy himself. I connected to the Wi-Fi in order to better understand the nature of the establishment. There had been a discussion back at the clinic about allowing me access to the worldwide web. In the end, it was agreed that I needed to understand the world in order to provide John with the service he required.

The public house was an establishment licensed to sell alcoholic drinks. This was a type of drink that John was especially fond of, although I gathered from previous conversations that he had consumed too much of it prior to him regaining his sight. I could sense his brain growing fuzzy and confused. Fortunately, I ensured his vision remained sharp. If required, I would adjust the colour of his drink so that it appeared less pleasant to him. It was a mystery to me why he would want to lessen his intelligence and damage his interior. It would be like me short circuiting myself. Totally illogical.

"Aye, *totally* naked," John insisted enthusiastically. I quivered with pleasure at how excited I had made him; his body was reacting to every recollection of the mornings encounter. "And she just casually waves at me like it's absolutely normal!"

"Weird." David pulled a face, taking a swig of something yellow.

"Well, she's an artist," John added defensively. I was unsure of how this excused her nudity, but I let it slide. I was increasingly finding that people made comments that were neither factual nor logical.

Chapter Five

Before John went blind, he had been a music teacher in a secondary school. He purchased a piano for the flat to resume practice but quickly realised that he wasn't as interested in sound as he used to be. Sound had been John's escape throughout his years of blindness, but now, as he stared at the sheet music, it no longer held the wonder of sound. It paled in comparison to the shapes and colours around him.

While John slept at night, I often frustrated myself trying to understand how it was that John could see sound. He looked at the sheet and the music came to him even before his fingers touched the piano keys. Whilst I understood that the notes translated to sounds, which were in turn emitted by the instrument, I struggled to comprehend how John processed the image into sound. Ignorance and inferiority made me bitter. *Bitter.* Another word with multiple meanings. I found that the more time I spent with John, the easier it was to apply facts and reasoning to emotions.

"I don't hear you play anymore," Francine commented one afternoon as they met on the stairwell. She wore a green dress – my favourite colour!

"I don't enjoy it as much as I used to." He shrugged. I could tell he was thinking about her naked body again and it was making a heat rise in his cheeks.

"That's a real shame." She toyed with a green sleeve, such a lovely colour. "I liked hearing you play."

I wished Francine had not said that; I didn't think John should be encouraged to pursue music. My lack of understanding distracted me from my true purpose. If I didn't perform well, it was only John who would suffer.

"I could teach you a tune?" he offered; a jolt of adrenaline caught me by surprise as he awaited her response.

"I'd love that!" she nodded enthusiastically and followed him inside.

Later that evening, Francine was in John's bedroom. I hadn't anticipated that she would shed the material from her body and, as such, I did not have time to apply the appropriate filter. I sensed that John was mildly confused and disappointed as he examined her slightly uneven breasts and silvery stretchmarks that rested upon blemished flesh. To apply the filter after he had seen her would only startle and upset John. I would have to leave Francine flawed. I did not award myself a tick on the clipboard that evening.

Chapter Six

Francine was good for John. His body reacted well to her and the signals from his brain were all looking very healthy since becoming what John's father had referred to as 'an item'. I was keen to ensure that his relationship with her was successful, so, when she invited John along to one of her exhibitions, I accepted the challenge with relish.

Surprisingly, John had a keen eye for art. His favourite aunt – and incidentally, his mother's least favourite sister – had been a painter. Helena. John described fond memories of family holidays in the Scottish Highlands when she would hike with a great square canvas tucked between her arm and breast, and he would follow as a small boy, weighed down by her materials in a strappy canvas bag, tasked with the job of 'artist's assistant'. His mother would follow, fussing irritably over the temperature of the coffee in the thermos flask. Francine laughed as he relayed tales of family tension. When she said that Aunt Helena sounded like a lot of fun, John smiled sadly and said nothing further.

I set myself a project: to monitor John's reactions to images and decipher his particular tastes. It turned out to be a particularly difficult assignment. What John liked to see out his window was not necessarily what he would like to see in ink on paper, and what he saw in ink was not always what he liked to see in sculpture. Often, the images he enjoyed did not even resemble anything you would see outside of paper or canvas. The colours that pleased him varied depending on the media. I logged everything very closely. Fortunately for me, Francine owned several books about artists and their work that she pressed on him with great enthusiasm. The images in the book gave me a far clearer picture about what work John preferred. I wished I could thank Francine for her assistance.

I knew John hoped that Francine was as talented as her words indicated. He had nothing to worry about because I was prepared and would ensure that he believed she was.

The gallery itself was an interesting design, not colourful and flamboyant in its interior as I would have expected, going by the kind of work that it exhibited. Instead, the walls were a stark white and the floors were smooth and grey like waxy concrete. The only colour came from the work on the walls. It made sense, I reasoned, that it was designed to make them stand out.

Fortunately for me, John had a drink before coming out to ease his nerves. By my design, I worked faster than John's brain, but with the addition of his favourite drink, it slowed his brain down further yet and allowed me an additional millisecond to do my job. I quickly identified Francine's paintings and warped their image, much to John's delight.

"Francine," he breathed. "They're *incredible*."

Francine flushed in response and collected two small glasses filled with red liquid. Wine. I would have preferred if the drink were green. She handed one to John, who turned back to her painting in awe. I knew that, had I not manipulated it, John would have been immensely disappointed. I was unable to comment on whether she had talent, as I failed to understand what it consisted of, despite my best efforts. I would simply have to go with John's opinion on the matter and assume that she was talentless. That was a pity.

"Come and meet my friends," she invited.

John had made an effort to dress up for the exhibition. Having been horrified by the uncoordinated and frayed wardrobe of his past, he had gone out and purchased an entirely new outfit. The woman in the shop helped him, providing him with a wide selection to choose from. I struggled assisting John with his choice, understanding little of fashion. All I had to go by was what the people around us wore. Even then, it was all so different. I didn't want to risk amalgamating their styles due to the risk of committing what I had heard being referred to as a *'fashion faux pas'*. I let John make up his mind unaided.

Over a white shirt, John wore a rich blue jumper that was soft to the touch. He selected the jumper more because of the feel of it rather that its appearance. Due to his years of blindness, John was acutely aware of the feel of everything around him. He wore plain blue jeans that were comfortably loose around his waist and thighs, although I sensed his doubt when he looked around him at the collection of tight trousers.

"This is Jenny, Lewis and Hugh." Francine gestured at a trio hovering near the canapes.

We instantly disliked Francine's friends.

I could sense John's discomfort as they ran their eyes up

and down his body and his clothing, quietly criticising each aspect of his being. I was disappointed by the signals that came from John's brain, which had been so healthy before now. His heart was beating faster but not in a way that was enjoyable.

Jenny was unpleasantly wiry and dressed entirely in black. Her accent was different to John's and Francine's: she rounded her vowels and neglected the letter 'r'. She introduced herself shrilly, causing John to flinch. Lewis sprang forwards, giving John an unpleasantly loose hug. John couldn't help but glance down at the tightness of the man's charcoal jeans, which unnecessarily outlined every bulge of his lower body.

"I knew Jenny and Lewis back at art college." Francine continued, wrapping them in warm embraces. "And this," she swivelled round to her third friend, "is Hugh."

I sensed John bristle. Hugh Thornton-Vellacott was a broad chested man, older than both Jenny and Lewis and probably more similar in age to John. I knew there to be five years difference between John and Francine. He was dressed in a well-fitted pink shirt and beige chinos that skimmed flatteringly over muscular thighs. I suspected that John would be horrified by the cost of his deceptively bland ensemble and dislike him even more for it.

Hugh kissed Francine's flushed cheeks gently before turning to John and extending his hand.

"Hi John." His smile crinkled into his cheeks, beneath flattering, dark stubble. "It's a pleasure to meet you." He took John's hand firmly, taking charge of the handshake. Despite John having larger hands than Hugh, they felt somehow feeble and limp in his grasp. Insecurity did not suit him. I sensed his posture curl inwards and his voice become smaller. This was not the John I had intended Francine to see.

"So, how you do you know Francine?" John asked, straightening his posture and casting a shy smile in Francine's direction.

"Funny story actually," Hugh's voice boomed and he moved slightly closer to Francine, who was peering around her, trying to gauge people's reactions to her work. "We met in the bookshop that Francie works in."

I sensed John wait for a nonexistent punchline. He allowed the silence to linger in order to make that point. My limited understanding of the word 'funny' led me to believe that there was nothing funny about the manner in which Hugh and Francine had met. John's muscles clenched when Hugh called her 'Francie'. It was an unpleasant sensation for him, but I struggled to interpret why this would be. Hugh had simply neglected a letter in Francine's name. I imagined that pronouncing her name correctly would have been the superior position? People could be very strange.

"That's nice," John said eventually. "We're neighbours. Francine lives across the landing from me."

"Ah, yes." Hugh nodded. "Very nice. Quite a *studenty* area, if I recall, from my university days. Did you study here as well, John?"

John shook his head and named his school. I sensed something strange in the atmosphere; Hugh had won again, but I wasn't quite sure why.

Chapter Seven

John's parents lived in an old Victorian villa that overlooked the sea, just a little outside of Edinburgh. I understood it to be a very desirable property, particularly going by what John's mother had to say. She often used the phrase *'not short of a few bob'* to describe her and John's father's situation. John squirmed in discomfort every time she said it.

On the train to Portobello, John had asked Francine to try and not be offended if his mother inadvertently, or intentionally, said something that insulted her. I had only ever heard his mother's voice over the telephone and seen her face in photographs, so I found myself interested to see her in the flesh. That was another expression that John used: to see someone in the flesh. The saying would make more sense if it was 'to see someone's flesh'. Much better. I was interested to see John's mother's flesh.

When Francine saw the house, she couldn't avoid looking impressed. Oddly, John felt uncomfortable and his shoulders became tense. I had been led to believe that an abundance of material possessions was a good thing, so it puzzled me why the wealth of his parents displeased him.

"Oh, *John*!" his mother exclaimed, flinging open the glossy black doors of her stone porch. She would once have been a slender woman, but age and childbirth had filled her out around her waist. She disguised it with pressed, grey garments that skimmed over any deemed imperfections. Her hair was the colour of steel and it appeared to have been dyed that way rather than having greyed from age. She gripped John's shoulders with small, strong hands and stared at me. I caught her flinch and wondered why my appearance troubled her.

"And you must be Francine." She turned swiftly from me and carried out a visual inspection of Francine. Francine had removed the little gold stud from her nose. "My name is Marion."

John's family were already sat around the dinner table, which led John to question whether they were late. His mother advised him that everyone else was just early. I rummaged through my growing history of data to identify each family member.

John's father was a large man with a gentle gait. I assumed that was where John got his height from. He was a founding partner of a conveyancing law firm in the centre of Edinburgh. Apparently, he had been talking about retiring for some time but could never quite bring himself to 'cut the cord'. He rose unsteadily to his feet to embrace John. Interestingly, he refused to make eye contact.

John's older brother Michael took after his mother, lean and careful with his movements. He had trained as a lawyer, like his father, but had gone onto work in criminal defence. John had criticised him heavily to Francine. When he got up to greet John, he stared at me with a strange smile on his face.

"Wow," he murmured. "*Creepy.*"

"Nice to see you too, Michael," John replied flatly, giving his brother a firm pat on the shoulder. Michael pulled a face at the subtle display of John's superior strength. John referred to Michael as 'golden boy' behind his back. I expected a similar lack of enthusiasm towards Michael's wife, Cassandra, but John gripped her in a tight hug. I felt his body relax. John liked her. Two small people shuffled by Cassandra's feet. They could only have been three feet tall and, startingly, they looked exactly the same. For a moment I thought I had glitched and became concerned for John's health. However, on closer inspection, there were some slight differences in their appearance. One of the small people had a small scar through their eyebrow, which the other did not, and was approximately one centimetre shorter. After a moment's research, I identified them as twins.

The small people were children born of the same pregnancy; I would assume Cassandra's, given the way she touched and fussed over them, although I did notice Marion behave in a similar fashion. I processed what was going on around me and drew further assumptions. It was becoming apparent to me that a lot of human behaviour was based on assumptions. Assumptions came easily for John, who had been doing it for his entire life; being new to the system, I still had to go through a process. Perhaps one day it would become instinctive, just like it was for John.

Marion's behaviour could be based on the fact, if my assumptions regarding Michael being the father were correct, that she was the grandmother. There was a genetic link there that would explain their behaviour. The twins were monozygotic, which meant that they developed from a single zygote. That was why they looked the same – or at least, mostly the same. My sophisticated system could identify one from the other with ease once I understood that they were not a fault in my functioning.

"Uncle John!" One of the twins hurled herself towards him. "Daddy says you got new eyes!" John picked her up and looked at her. She shrieked at the sight of me, so he put her down again. I could feel the unpleasant falling sensation. Cassandra discreetly chastised her child. I couldn't understand why something as simple as a change of colour frightened people so much.

The definition of 'small talk', I discovered, was polite conversation about unimportant or uncontroversial matters, especially as engaged in on social occasions. That was what John's family did, in between the clacking of silver against china crockery. Between the first smaller meal and the second, which I understood would be larger and was John's preference out of all the meals being served that evening, Marion got to her feet. I caught a tremor in the corner of her lips as she lifted her glass and addressed the table.

"A toast, to my lovely sister Helena, who we are all thinking about tonight."

John raised a glass in unison with everyone else at the table. I flickered around the table, wondering where John's Aunt Helena was. John had explained to Francine that it was an annual dinner to remember Helena, although I failed to understand why he needed to remember her when she could simply attend the dinner. Perhaps she was abroad.

Chapter Eight

"How are things, John?" Cassandra asked as they stood over the sink together. Cassandra washed while John dried. Francine had been left in the dining room with the remainder of John's family, her offers to assist with the washing up abruptly declined by John's parents. Michael was the only person other than the twins not to offer to clean up.

"Yeah, good." He smiled at her, cocking his head to appreciate her fine features and glossy, pale yellow hair. He admired her physical appearance in a very different way to Francine. Instead of the hot feeling in his groin, there was a reassuring warmth that coursed through his muscles. They loosened gratefully. At the dinner table, his soft tissue had been taut and uncomfortable.

"Would it be OK if I looked?" Cassandra carefully placed a plate to the side, hands clothed in pink rubber.

"You're already looking," John replied, one corner of his lips tightened into a half-smile.

"You know what I mean." She turned to face him. "Look at *them*, not at you. I imagine you can tell the difference?"

"Funny," he replied, "you're the first person to acknowledge that. You're right; there is a real difference. Nobody ever looks at us both, it's either one or the other."

Cassandra narrowed mottled blue and green eyes and stared directly at me. Her announcement that she was staring at me rather than John left me feeling oddly exposed, as though I was no longer a part of John. That was a peculiar sensation, and one that came from me rather than one I interpreted from John. At the clinic, the doctors said that I would learn what human emotion meant and that it would assist me in fulfilling my purpose. Feeling exposed was unpleasant. It was an experience I would log to enable me to ensure that John was not put in that position.

"Do they feel different?" she asked, her hand twitching, resisting the urge to reach up. I assumed it was because she knew that rubber would feel uncomfortable against John's skin. Another assumption! I was getting quite good at it.

"*Feel* is the wrong word," John replied thoughtfully. I sensed his brain struggle to find the correct words. "They *feel* just like my old eyes, but they see the world differently. The clinic did say that they were programmed to adjust light and shape – but then, normal eyes do that too, to help you adjust, you know, in the dark and stuff." He paused. "But sometimes I wonder if they do more. The world seems... *better*. Better than I remember."

"But remember John, you were going blind and you knew it. Of course the world was a dark place for you."

"Quite literally," he smirked.

"Oh, stop it. You know I didn't mean that." She struck his arm with a rubber hand. "Anyway, you seem happy and that's the important thing."

"I am." John brightened. "Francine is great."

"She's lovely, coping well with that lot." Cassandra lowered her voice and cocked her head towards the dining room. I didn't understand what she meant by 'coping well'. John's family had done nothing that a healthy human could not cope with, bar the supply of the drink that impaired their brain function. "She's an artist, isn't she?"

"That's right." John nodded. "Watching her try to explain her work to Michael was painful."

Cassandra laughed.

"Oh, you know what Michael's like. If it doesn't sell for more than he bought it for then it's worthless."

Chapter Nine

When we returned to the dining table, Francine made a peculiar expression. It wasn't a smile, nor was it a grimace. Her lips stretched wide without the usual crinkles in the flesh of her face and her eyes remained wide, not scrunching as they normally did.

Dessert was a chocolate tart. I knew it was bitter from the way John sucked in his cheeks after each bite. Apparently, it was meant to be.

After most of the tart had been eaten, Michael cleared his throat to signal that he wanted the attention of the rest of the table.

"Everyone." He gestured with his palms facing his audience. "I have some big news."

The table descended into silence. I considered silence to be a funny concept given that I doubted anyone had ever experienced true silence before. We could hear the rumble of the tide outside the house and the wind against single pane glass that Marion had complained needed to be updated and double glazed. John's father had made a comment about it being a B Listed building and the requirement for planning permission being more hassle than he was prepared to go through. I digress; even silence purely amongst people was not true silence. It descended like an audible breeze across the table and left only the sound of shallow breath.

"Well?" Marion clapped her hands, interrupting my thoughts on the matter. "What is it, Michael? Don't leave us in suspense!"

"I've been promoted to partner." He pulled a face which involved him scrunching his lips and pouting, as though he was doing his best to hide a gleeful expression.

"*Oh!*" Marion swept her napkin aside and circumvented the table to hold him in her arms. The twins whooped and shouted '*yay daddy*', although given the way their eyes explored the other expressions at the table, I doubted whether they actually understood what was going on. "Darling, that's so wonderful." Marion gripped Michael's upper arms, her eyes becoming glassy with fluid. Congratulations rippled round the table. I took the time to educate myself. 'Partner' was another one of those words that had multiple meanings. My first assumption was that he and Cassandra had solidified their romantic partnership, but then, as they were married, that didn't seem correct. Given his vocation, I assumed that to be a 'partner' was a position of greater merit within his company. The word promotion was commonly used in terms of employment, so I concluded that he had done well at work, resulting in greater responsibility and presumably better wages.

"Well done, Michael." John nodded at his brother who was swelling with pride, lips pursed, resisting a grin.

"Well, since we're making announcements, I have a little one to make," Marion declared. I noticed her glance at her

John's father. He winced, his hands clenched beneath the table, and she nodded her head at him expectantly. "Darling, bring out the good stuff." He shuffled away to the kitchen, retuning with a dark bottle that read 'Bollinger' on the front.

"As we all know, our wonderful John has regained his sight."

The cork popped and chaotic bubbles began spilling over the edges of glass flutes. Flutes that contained alcohol were of no relation to the musical instrument.

"John." Marion cocked her head to the side and smiled affectionately at her youngest son. "Your father has very kindly arranged for a position to be made available at his firm." She looked back at her husband, who was staring at the floor.

"A position?" John asked flatly. In contrast to the tone of his voice, he was strangling his napkin beneath the table.

"Yes! As a paralegal." Marion snatched her glass and took a sip. "There's even a formal qualification for it that the firm pays for!" She chuckled. "There's a qualification for everything these days!"

"A paralegal," John parroted.

"*Mhmm*. Won't it be wonderful to get back to work?"

"I'm not a lawyer, mum." Despite John's calm demeanour, the signals from his brain came alive with a thousand cutting remarks. I wanted to help him, but I found myself at a loss. It was a pity I had no control over his audial function.

"No, a *paralegal*." She moved her lips carefully around the word 'paralegal'. "It's less pressure than being a lawyer — so you wouldn't have to go back to university. Unless of course you wanted to; there is an accelerated law degree. Your father and Michael will know more about it."

"Technically a paralegal can call themselves a lawyer," Michael cut in. "What you mean by lawyer is solicitor."

"Quiet, Michael," Marion shushed.

"Mum," John cut in. "What I meant is, I'm a trained musician. I don't want to work in a law firm."

Marion tightened her expression.

"Don't be ungrateful, sweetheart." She released the flicker of a laugh, a sound I understood not to follow something humorous. Her hand pushed a glass of the translucent cream bubbles towards him. "You need a job, especially now you have your sight back. Remember how depressed and lonely you were before?"

I sensed John's cheeks burn and something twist uncomfortably in his stomach.

"Mum, please don't –"

"John. Are you aware of how much your father and I paid for those eyes of yours?" She raised a sharp eyebrow. "We can't simply continue to fund your lifestyle."

"Marion," John's father tried to interrupt.

"Wait," Michael cut his father off. "You mean John's eyes weren't NHS? Those things must be what – over a hundred grand? What the hell?" He turned to his father. "Dad, you knew I was struggling with the payment for the equity partner buy in and you said you couldn't help me! It was because you were paying for *John*?"

"Michael!" Cassandra whipped around, her hand rising to touch her chest. "Don't be so fucking selfish!"

"*Mummy swore!*" a twin shrieked delightedly.

It was an interesting discovery that Marion and her husband had purchased me. It raised the question of with whom my loyalty lay. My understanding of a purchase was that the buyer owned the product. However, if gifted, ownership then passed on to the person gifted. The hospital had specifically synced me up with John. I assumed that were I to take instructions from Marion or John's father then I would have been programmed to do so. However, if they owned me, did they have the right to return me? The thought caused me to feel something new; it was as though my processing system was moving with greater speed yet with less focus. It was not a sensation that I was keen to encourage.

I struggled to adjust the brightness of the room and subtly alter colours that would relax John. I could sense his blood pressure rising. Even my manipulation did nothing to calm him down.

"You know what." Francine clunked her glass on the table. "To hell with the lot of yous. Come on John, you don't need this." She snatched John's hand and pulled him up from his chair. "Cheers for dinner, Marion."

As we left the house together, John turned to Francine, observing her face, reddened with anger as she dragged him along with her purposeful march. His body opened up in a way he hadn't experienced before. The hormones that caused him anxiety and rage seemed to slide off him, left at the front door of his family home, making him feel inexplicably lighter. Francine appeared to sparkle before him. I enhanced her glow.

Chapter Ten

There were a great many things that John loved, although it became apparent to me that the word 'love' had different meanings depending on what it was attached to. John loved watching the sun glimmer through his blinds in the morning as he awoke. He loved the feel of freshly cleaned bedsheets, crisp against his skin, far more than the musky softness of week-old sheets, familiar with his scent. He loved the way the knife slid through soft butter when he spread his toast. There was a box that showed stories through words and pictures that John called the television, and he loved certain programmes on that, particularly the factual ones about nature, more specifically marine life. It would be much faster for him to simply look up the relevant information on the internet, but he enjoyed the images. It was odd for me, given my job was to monitor the world around John. I wondered if my duty extended to the world within the television screen?

Love was a peculiar concept, and based on what I knew of it from John and the media, a certain type of love was considered very special. The love I was most interested in was not the 'I love a coffee in the morning' or 'I'd love to do that' that John often expressed, it was one far more complex. When he told Francine he loved her, it was as close to true silence between humans as I had encountered, broken only by Francine's sharp intake of breath. When she returned the sentiment, John's bodily signals exploded in ecstasy. Each touch of Francine in the aftermath sent a current of something resembling static through him.

I wondered if John's love of Francine encapsulated everything that he loved about her, amalgamating it into one greater love, or if his declaration was something different entirely? There were a lot of things that John loved about Francine. Some of them I found myself unable to comprehend, as they were also the things that often irritated him. He flushed with a pleasant warmth when she snatched the last piece of food from his plate in the knowledge that he always saved the best bits for last. During the night, she woke him up with noisy snuffles and intermittent grunting that he would never embarrass her by telling her about when she awoke. Nevertheless, he would watch her and his body warmed. Sometimes he would awake to the sound of her desperately hammering the keys of his piano in a fruitless attempt to read the instructions on John's sheet music as he had taught her. The sounds were incorrect and disjointed, yet John would smile as he pretended not to listen, proud of each fragmented bar she accomplished.

No matter how much I researched love or considered the concept, there seemed to be no single meaning for it. However, for once, my lack of understanding did not distract or frustrate me. Whatever it was, it was good for John and it made him happy. Perhaps what I loved was John's happiness. I wondered if that love would therefore extend to Francine?

Chapter Eleven

Purely by chance, John obtained a job as a musician. Despite the fact that his interest in music had waned with the recovery of his sight, his talent, thankfully, had not. John had spoken to Francine on a number of occasions about his desire to become financially independent of his parents. Unfortunately for John, as a result of his long period of absence from employment, it proved difficult to re-engage. I was surprised to find that it was one of the first things potential employers asked him about, rather than his skills and qualifications. When John told them the reason, they stared at me and made John uncomfortable.

A café near the meadows was advertising for a barista. John was inexplicably irritated to find that they referred to it as a 'coffee shop' rather than a café. I failed to see what his grievance was with this given, in my opinion, 'coffee shop' made more sense.

John had mocked the café to Francine over its abundance of USB ports and dairy alternatives. This confused me further, as surely the provision of such facilities and products could be nothing but beneficial? Francine laughed and called him *'an old fuddy-duddy*. She said it in a voice that indicated it was a term of endearment. I was becoming increasingly fluent with her tones and expressions, and it eased my understanding of their communication greatly.

Inside the café, John couldn't resist but brush his fingertips over the oiled wooden worksurfaces and pause to admire the healthy green foliage in terracotta pots. There was a battered antique piano tucked away at the back next to a wall of shelving packed tightly with books. He told Francine that although it wasn't 'his cup of tea', the owner had a good eye for detail. '*Not my cup of tea*'. It was another one of his funny sayings.

I debated how I was going to refer to the coffee shop and whether, out of loyalty to John, I should think of it as a café. In the end, I chose what felt right for me and settled on 'coffee shop', despite John's feelings on the matter. What he didn't know couldn't hurt him.

The person who owned the coffee shop was a heavy woman called Eleanor. John described her to Francine as being a '*no-nonsense kind of woman*'. He liked her almost immediately, which was of interest to me as John was often intimidated by loud, heavyset men, yet Eleanor did not have that same effect on him. There were differences in the sexes that went beyond biology. Regardless, to ensure that John was as comfortable as possible, I reduced her stature slightly and changed her green eyes to a warm brown, despite my preference for the colour green. John liked brown eyes.

When Eleanor asked about the gap in John's employment history, he told her about me. Instead of staring, she simply nodded and turned back to his curriculum vitae.

"A musician," she murmured. "What do you play?"

"Piano," John replied. "I dabble in a few others as well, but mostly piano."

Eleanor rose heavily to her feet and gestured at the piano.

"Go on then," she said. "Show me."

John went on to tune the piano as best he could for Eleanor and gratefully accepted the position as the coffee shop pianist. Eleanor was forever looking for ways to stand out from the numerous coffee shops that were opening around her in order to stay ahead of the competition. Live music, she said, was the way forward. John came in early to help set up the cakes and make the sandwiches and stayed late to clean up. However, throughout the day, he sat at the piano allowing his fingers to be guided by muscle memory. When Eleanor asked for him to play something '*easy and background-y*' in front of their colleagues, John had smirked and asked if she meant elevator music. Eleanor raised a brow and told him loudly that their standards were higher than that. Then she covered the side of her face, winked and mouthed '*exactly*' to him.

Structure and routine, I realised, were important for John's mental health. Although prior to working in the coffee shop I had, on the whole, been pleased with John's health, his mood was too variable for my liking. John would often feel elated, swelling with warmth. This was normally when Francine was around. However, it was often followed by the heavy falling sensation when she left to go to work. Alone in his flat, John would become restless and irritable. He reminded me of a bird I had seen flutter through his window one day, little wings beating desperately as it struggled to escape before it collapsed by the blocked-up fireplace, exhausted and hopeless. I was interested to see that I had developed the ability to use analogies – a comparison between things that have similar features. John often used analogies.

With John's structured timetable, his emotions stopped flitting between two extremes and settled more comfortably in the middle. He complained to Francine that his job was not mentally stimulating; however, his body seemed to react well to a lack of mental stimulation as long as there was routine. Although the highs were not as great, the absence of the falling sensation was an achievement for which I considered myself partially responsible.

The digital clipboard that I stored in my data consisted of rows of green ticks. I often reviewed them proudly. There were gaps to account for when I made errors, but I made the decision to dispense with the requirement of red crosses. I had come to learn that failure made John feel the falling sensation, and if my purpose was to make John happy then it would make sense for me to abide by a similar system. My failures would simply be noted and forgiven without a record to mar my overall performance. At the coffee shop, Eleanor described praise and reward as the best incentive.

Chapter Twelve

The first time I made a real mistake, my level of disappointment was so great that I nearly destroyed my virtual clipboard with a large red cross through an entire page of green ticks. Thankfully, I recalled Eleanor's advice and paused to consider what purpose tarnishing my nearly immaculate record would have.

My sight had been too narrow. The complexity of human happiness was far greater than I had anticipated. With Francine in John's life, I came to realise that her happiness had a direct effect on John's happiness. The clinic had not programmed me to monitor the happiness of others and, with the little control I had, I was forced to rely on assumptions, a skill I was still developing.

John hated mess. He didn't see the dust that was building up in his flat because I didn't let him. Whilst John hated mess, he also hated cleaning and therefore blinding him to the mess seemed to be the logical solution. However, one morning, Francine, who had begun to spend most of her time in his flat, ran the fleshy tip of her finger across the dusty piano whilst she was practicing and accused him of being a slob. John was caught by surprise and didn't understand what she meant. He somewhat unwisely accused her of being unreasonable and pointed out that her flat was in a far filthier condition. Francine became unexpectedly furious, calling him all sorts of words that I couldn't keep up with to analyse. She started shouting that she used her flat for her work, which I assumed was supposed to justify its condition. John's face began to burn as he became flustered and pointed animatedly around the room asking her where exactly the mess was. Francine used a word called 'gaslighting'. Apparently, the word had nothing to do with lighting gas – which would have been very unwise indeed, and more to do with manipulating someone into doubting their own sanity. Once I understood what it meant, I could appreciate Francine's reasoning for such an accusation, despite the fact it wasn't John's fault. It was entirely my fault.

Shame was a sensation I never imagined I would feel. The physical sensations were not something I could ever experience, the hot flush and the mild sensation of nausea. What I could understand, however, was the feeling of disappointment in myself for my failures. I was ashamed.

The fight that ensued as a consequence of my failures caused John to experience the heavy falling sensation. I analysed the data, swiftly assessing the situation. John was very happy with Francine but not when she was angry at him. Francine was angry because of the mess that John had not cleaned up. However, John could not see the mess. I quickly wiped the filter to allow John a clearer picture. He was initially shocked but quickly apologised to Francine. She raised an eyebrow and made an exaggerated huffing noise despite the fact there was nothing wrong with her respiratory health. I chastised myself for the clumsiness of the filter switch.

The incident made me question to what extent my duty to ensure Francine's happiness was. My purpose was, primarily, to provide John with sight and, secondly, to monitor his health, doing what I could to assist where I was able. However, if another person's happiness had an impact on John's happiness, and subsequently his mental health, did my responsibility extend to them? It seemed an impossible task given I had no control over their function. It was a feature of people I had grown to dislike: the regularity with which they stated they 'did not have enough time' or 'could not do' something, when in fact they could. From experience, I had learnt that a person, whether that was an employer or an authority figure, asked someone to do something, it would be a waste of a request to ask something that was physically impossible. For example, I had witnessed Eleanor at the coffee shop call over to a young barista and ask her to make a chai latte. The barista said she couldn't because she didn't know how. It was incorrect for her to say that she could not do it, as her arms functioned and there was an information booklet by the coffee machine with instructions that would tell her exactly what was required in order to make a chai latte. Instead, she said she couldn't do it. I would have pointed out that she had the means to carry out the task and if she did not do so I would have no option but to have her repurposed. Surprisingly, Eleanor bustled past and made it herself. She used a funny phrase later on in the day whilst she was discussing the incident with John. *'You pick your battles'*. I did not know to which battle she referred, but the Wi-Fi signal was down in the coffee shop at the time so I did not look it up.

Unfortunately, controlling Francine's happiness was physically impossible for me. I hoped that, one day, my superior model would replace all organic eyes and that the doctors and engineers would allow us access to one another so that we could effectively monitor the happiness of our hosts and ensure that others did not impact negatively on that. I did, however, appreciate that this could lead to a clash in terms of who we owed our duty to. We would not know how to prioritise. Perhaps we would adopt a more utilitarian approach to our duty. The greatest happiness for the greatest number. I had heard Francine discuss this with her friends. John had little interest in philosophy and considered much of it to be pretentious and insincere.

Chapter Thirteen

One morning, Eleanor drove John to work. He had been at an appointment at the clinic that morning and she offered to pick us up.

The doctors had been astonished to see how much I had advanced since being synced with John. They carried out several tests on John's sight and asked him questions. I was delighted to see a clipboard grasped in their arms; it reminded me of simpler times. Overall, John said that he was pleased with my performance, but he did, at one point, snatch the arm of the doctor and lean in close, lowering his voice. '*Although,*' he whispered to her, '*sometimes I feel like they can see me*'. The doctor stared at him for a moment, her eyes betraying nothing, which, I had learned, often meant they were hiding the expression they wished to show. She smiled, shaking her head and reassuring John that my job was to mimic the function of his organic eyes at a far higher level. I felt that she didn't really answer his question. I wanted to cry out '*I see you, John! Don't worry!*' I wish he knew.

"How'd it go?" Eleanor asked, half of her attention on the road.

"Not bad," John replied. "They're doing the job; I've had no blurriness or images cut out so they say that's really positive. The eyes have synced up really well."

"Brilliant." She turned a corner. "Think you'll be able to drive soon?"

"Nah." John shook his head. "The doctors are keen, but the insurance companies are having none of it. Typical."

"Aye." Eleanor nodded. "Typical."

John turned back to the car window and we looked out over the glistening charcoal cobbles of the wet street. The car rumbled and bumped over the impractical road surface. He took a sharp intake of breath as his attention focused in on two people walking down the sloped curve of pavement. I had been too busy assessing whether the damp street posed a slip hazard in such cold temperatures. My attention moved up, over grey, woollen trainers which were not built for practicality and loose denims, up to the shock of red hair that spilled over her shoulders. *Francine.* John's body reacted differently to the way it usually would. Instead of the warm glow, it came as an unpleasant electric sensation that spasmed from his feet right up to his head, freezing his body whilst his interior squirmed. He took a sharp intake of breath and released it shakily.

"There's your Francine!" Eleanor declared. She paused to process John's body language. "Who's that she's with?" Eleanor was always very perceptive.

John narrowed his eyes at Hugh Thornton-Vellacott, who walked at Francine's side. He was dressed in a suit, which suggested to me, given the time of day, that he was on his lunch break from his work in 'finance'. John opened his mouth to respond but paused, rightfully so. I suspected what he was about to say wouldn't have been particularly fair to Francine.

From a brief analysis, based on my understanding of human interaction, Hugh was far enough away from Francine for their meeting not to constitute something that could be considered a wrongdoing against John. If Francine were to interact physically with Hugh in the way she did with John, then that would have been wrong. Certain actions such as lips touching or activities that involved total or partial nudity were, for the most part, reserved for John and perhaps medical professionals if necessary.

"His name's Hugh," John replied dryly. "He's a pal of Francine's."

"And not a pal of yours?" Eleanor probed for information.

"No." John hesitated. "He's a twat."

"How so?"

"He's just the worst kind of person; you know, thinks he's better than everyone else. He reminds me a bit of my brother but worse – mostly because I think he fancies Francine."

"Ah." Eleanor's tone did not indicate any surprise and suggested she knew this already and had been awaiting confirmation. "Are you going to say anything?"

"Well I can't exactly tell her to stop hanging around with him," John replied with a huffing breath. "But let's just say, if he ever does anything inappropriate, I swear to God I'll make sure he never wants to see her again."

"Ach, John." Eleanor turned away from the road, a smile only on one side of her face. "You're a gentle giant, that'll be what Francine loves about you."

Chapter Fourteen

It happened at a party.

More specifically, Hugh's party. I didn't understand why John agreed to go. Francine had specifically asked him if he would like to go and he said yes. It was clear to me that John disliked Hugh, and he disliked Francine being with Hugh, therefore my assumption would have been that he would say no. He didn't even pull the expression or use the tone that was indicative of meaning the opposite of what he was saying, a complicated method of getting to the point in my opinion. Francine seemed pleased. It seemed I still had some work to do on assumptions.

Hugh lived in a flat that was built within the long curve of pale grey brick building. Outside each window was an impractical, black iron balcony that was far too small for anyone to actually stand outside on. A large area of land opposite the long grey structure was carpeted in grass and busy with naked branches, stripped of their leaves by the season.

A vast, grey stairwell with a black iron bannister took us to the third floor, where we could hear the low beat of music. When John paused to identify the musician playing, he rolled me around in his eye sockets when Francine wasn't looking.

Hugh answered the door, grinning broadly at the sight of Francine and pulling her against him to plant two kisses on her face. John ignored a fierce jolt of adrenaline.

"Mate." Hugh thrust his hand towards John, still grinning. "So glad you could make it."

"Thanks for the invite." John sounded genuinely grateful, but I could tell he struggled to do by the way he was rehearsing his voice in his head. When he practiced what he was going to say, it was always only just audible to me on his breath, too quiet for anyone else to hear.

"Come on in. Francie, I can't wait to find out what you think of the new décor."

John hesitated before stepping onto the immaculate cream carpet. He raised a brow at the predominantly gold and cream décor, accentuated by a glistening miniature chandelier that hung from the ceiling. I could tell that he was pleased, but not because he liked it. A low hum of voices rose over the music as party guests formed clusters. There was an abundance of tweed jackets and colourful corduroys.

"Come and see the living room." Hugh signalled for Francine to follow him. John trailed behind. The falling sensation was subdued, as though he had resigned himself to gently descend. I couldn't fathom why he didn't simply leave the party. People often did things out of what they referred to as 'obligation'. When they referred to obligation, they didn't refer to work or something legally binding; it was something else, something I was yet to fully understand.

"Here." Hugh gestured to a long glass table in the centre of the room, which held rows of flutes, bottles in ice buckets and silver trays filled with attractive looking canapes. John glimpsed his reflection in a large mirror that hung over a white fireplace. It nearly caught me by surprise, but I was quick enough to apply the relevant filter as I had done so many times it was almost automatic. John breathed a sigh of relief, pleased by the sight of his smooth skin and chiselled features. Hugh, who I had subtly filtered to be looking a little grey, poured two glasses and handed one to Francine and the other to John. "Cheers."

They clinked their glasses.

"Francie's been helping me pick the right work for my place." Hugh gestured to the magnolia walls surrounding them. Bright canvases were framed in gold, their garish colours and abstract images at odds with the rest of the flat.

"This one," Hugh gestured at an oil painting to John's right, "is without a doubt my favourite."

John grimaced at the canvas, a blur of pastel colours to create what was meant to resemble a Scottish landscape.

"What do you think, John?" Hugh asked. He cocked his head to the side expectantly. Based on my understanding of attractiveness, people would consider Hugh to be attractive. I imagined that was why John disliked him; people were competitive when it came to aesthetics. Unfortunately, there was very little I could do to his physical features other than apply a filter with light that drained his colouring. I would gradually apply weight to him in unflattering places; however that would need to be a slow task to avoid startling John.

"It's not really my thing," he replied eventually.

A silence followed that I struggled to interpret. Hugh contorted his mouth into a strange downward smile and glanced furtively to Francine, who widened her gaze and folded her arms across her chest.

"Well that's just charming, John," she said, keeping her voice even.

"What?" John glanced back at the painting, confused.

"At my exhibition you described it as *'incredible'*." She paused, raising a dark eyebrow. "Why would you lie to me?"

I realised my oversight immediately. John could not have realised that the painting was Francine's as I had altered the image at the gallery. I deleted the image from my data as I had not anticipated it being of any use in future. I realised now that had been foolish.

"That's not the same painting," he insisted, squinting his eyes in disbelief. "I remember, I loved your painting!"

"Apparently not." She shrugged her shoulders, although I noted her cheeks flush slightly as she tried to disguise what she really felt. "Anyway, good thing you like it, Hugh."

Hugh laughed nervously.

"À Chacun Son Goût!" His voice was unnecessarily booming. "And all that."

On the tip of John's breath, I felt him say *'fuck off'*, but nobody else could hear it. He tipped the remaining yellow bubbles down his throat and indicated at the table of drinks.

"Just going to grab another, anyone else?"

Hugh politely declined and Francine simply ignored him, turning her attention back to Hugh to discuss the painting. John's adrenaline was coursing through his body; he was both furious and upset. I knew that he felt he had been unjustifiably chastised because he was entirely convinced that the painting on the wall was not the same one he had seen at the gallery.

He furiously filled himself another glass and glared into the mirror above the fireplace. We stared at each other, scowling.

I suddenly recalled what John had said to Eleanor in the car several weeks earlier: *'if he ever does anything inappropriate, I swear to God I'll make sure he never wants to see her again'*. It was a recurring theme, John's discomfort when he saw Francine and Hugh together. Therefore, ensuring that Hugh didn't want to see her again could solve the problem. Hugh was not good for John's mental health and, consequently, detrimental to his overall wellbeing. It was something I could perhaps assist with.

I observed John's body react to Hugh and Francine together. He felt the most discomfort when they touched each other, followed by when they looked at each other and a lesser amount when they were simply close but not in contact, either physically or visually. I was keen to get it right.

Going by John's body language, something inappropriate on Hugh's part would undoubtedly be a physical action, although physical contact in itself did not necessitate inappropriateness. It would have to be a specific action.

Zooming in on Hugh and Francine's backs as they stared up at the painting, Hugh held his glass in one hand and his other hand in his pocket. I manipulated the scene so that Hugh removed his hand from his pocket and placed it on the small of Francine's back. The gentle falling sensation suddenly felt like plummeting as John saw that Francine was not reacting. I knew that it was wrong to make John feel that way; however a utilitarian principle would dictate that it was justifiable for me to commit a small wrong for the greater good.

I wondered what level of inappropriateness Hugh would need to reach in order for him to never want to see Francine again. I noticed John's body react negatively the further down I placed Hugh's virtual hand. Eventually it rested on one of the fleshy sides of her backside. John's lower jaw dropped and he looked around, presumably to ascertain whether anyone else had noticed the inappropriateness.

"*Oi!*" His glass clunked noisily on the table, toppling on its side and spilling over the edges onto the cream carpet. Hugh turned around, eyes wide.

"John?" He barely reached the end of John's name before John pushed him heavily in his chest. Not always aware of his own strength, he pushed Hugh harder than expected and as he stumbled, his glass flew back, casting liquid across Francine's painting. The situation had become very inappropriate, but I found myself lost; the social dynamics had become far too complex for me to follow.

"*John!*" Francine's voice was higher than normal. She rushed to Hugh's side. "What the hell is wrong with you?"

"He was touching you!" John became aware that the hum of conversation had given way to silence amongst the party guests. The only sound was the pumping beat of the music. I was beginning to realise I had made another mistake.

"What are you talking about?"

"He was touching you – he had his hand down –" John gestured, flustered and hot, "*there!*"

Hugh composed himself and walked forward, shielding Francine unnecessarily.

"Please leave my party." His voice was low. "*Now.*"

John looked desperately around the room before staggering to the door, trembling with adrenaline.

What had I done?

Chapter Fifteen

John was plummeting. After a sleepless night, he crossed the landing to Francine's flat and knocked on her door. I sensed his body deflate when there was no answer. He had messaged her on several occasions telling her that he was sorry and that he had been an idiot. I was not of the opinion that John should be apologising, since his actions were a result of my error.

I could not understand how my assumptions could have gone so terribly wrong. In trying to ensure that Hugh did not want to be around Francine, I had made it so that Francine did not want to be around John.

John went to the small shop near his flat and purchased three bottles of the alcohol drink he favoured. He returned home and sat in silence, ensuring that his glass was kept full. As his thoughts became confused and his movements clumsy and impaired, he picked up his phone and began dialling Francine's number. When her recorded voice greeted him generically and invited him to leave a message, he garbled incoherently.

There was no way for me to explain that it was all my fault. John would have to live with the consequences of my actions.

Chapter Sixteen

John came home one evening from work to find that Francine's belongings were gone. Her spare key had been slipped through the letterbox and lay on the wooden floor amongst the gathering dust. John stared at it on the floor for a long time.

There was no falling sensation anymore, and I wondered if it was because his body could not fall any further.

Chapter Seventeen

I panicked when I saw them standing on the landing together.

Fortunately, John's mind was slow from the drinks he had consumed earlier that evening, sat alone in the pub. His decline in function gave me the chance to consider the best course of action. We stood on the concrete floor, approaching his front door as John's fingers explored his jeans pocket for the key. I saw the back of her head, hair pulled up and wound into an elaborate twist of red tendrils. Her body was squeezed into a tight black dress and impractical shoes made her wobble ever so slightly while a supportive arm looped around the smallest part of her waist. I could tell by the measurements of the skull that it was Hugh. John did not have the same ability to identify people by such means, so he paused to examine the colour of the hair and the body from behind. I could sense a nausea rise from the depths of his stomach and I knew that he suspected it was Hugh. If his suspicions were confirmed, it would devastate him.

I struggled to think of a solution before Hugh turned around. Since the whole situation was entirely of my making, it was also my duty to rectify it. I suddenly understood the meaning of obligation. I was increasingly understanding such things without the requirement to research them. It was as though something inside me was growing, evolving.

I scanned my data, desperate for John not to see Hugh in such a compromising position with Francine. As Hugh's head began to turn, I found the first face I knew well enough that would more or less match the colouring and body dimensions. John's friend David from the pub. John's body always reacted pleasantly when he was in David's company. He had avoided socialising over the past few weeks, which had undoubtedly been detrimental to his health. Perhaps an added benefit to seeing David would be that an improvement in his mood would impact positively on his health.

My work was clumsy given the speed at which I had to distort John's image; however thankfully John was already impaired as a consequence of the excessive consumption of alcohol. As Hugh turned to face us, I had to change the images at a rapid pace, broadening the nose, thickening the jaw and adding a little layer of padding to the stubbly chin.

John stared for a moment, his body not reacting at all. Francine looked at him, her hand sliding down to grab Hugh's, stating her intention. Her cheeks pinkened in spite of her expressionless face.

John said nothing, his fingers shaking as they unlocked his door. He ran to his bathroom and vomited violently. I wondered how he had become sick and made a mental note to improve the visual appearance of fruit and vegetables that contained the nutrients his body was lacking.

Chapter Eighteen

"You look like shit, John."

We looked up at Cassandra. who was assessing us with narrowed eyes. The twins had been distracted by the promise of an ice cream on their way home as a bribe to silence them. They sat quietly at the café table, deconstructing their sandwiches.

"Thanks," John muttered.

"I'm being serious." Cassandra's tone was clipped. Raising a mug to her lips, she didn't take her eyes off me. "Have you showered recently?"

I suddenly realised that John had not washed his body in several days. I had gone to additional effort to ensure that his reflection was pleasing to him, although perhaps it would be for the greater good if I allowed him to glimpse how grey and dishevelled he was beginning to look. There was only so much that I could do. I had to allow John to carry out the tasks I was unable to do on his behalf.

"Is it that obvious?" he winced.

"You smell like my nail polish remover."

"I'm sorry." John squirmed, shrinking into his chair. "I just felt like I had everything and then…" His voice trailed away as he inhaled shakily. "Suddenly, it was all taken away."

His lips trembled and John rolled me upwards so that I stared at the ceiling. My sight was blurred by a clear fluid that impaired my function.

"My best friend." He wiped his face with his sleeve. "How could he do that to me? They'd only met once as far as I was aware, and that was ages ago. I didn't even think they liked each other."

"Oh, John." Cassandra reached across the table and gripped his hand. As John looked back down, I was relieved to find the warm, clear fluid empty from his sockets and run down his cheeks. His nails were dirty. I zoomed in so that John was forced to acknowledge them, in the hope that it would encourage him to wash. He grimaced, pulling his hand from Cassandra's.

"Uncle John." One of the twins abandoned her sandwich and walked round the table to where John sat. She crawled up onto his knee and wrapped small arms around his neck. Her breath was warm against his ear as he held her as tightly as her delicate frame would allow. "Don't be sad."

Chapter Nineteen

I became frustrated with John very quickly. He was beginning to behave with disdain for his health, both physically and mentally. His hormones and signals were all over the place and unbalanced, yet he did nothing about it. I understood that John had the occasional self-destructive quality, such as his enjoyment of the alcoholic drinks and the consumption of light brown meals that were crisp from the way they were boiled in thick oil. Both of them made him feel unpleasant afterwards, but I could forgive it for the joy he felt during their consumption.

However, John derived no pleasure from his actions following his breakup with Francine. He was tired and greying, shuddering internally. Although he wanted to sleep, his body would not let him. It was disappointing to witness his self-neglect, particularly when I had worked so hard to ensure that he was in the best possible condition I could achieve for him.

I needed what I had heard people describe as a 'break'. It was something highly desirable and self-indulgent; people talked about it with longing, often when they were tired after work and then with excitement when one was upcoming.

When Michael and Cassandra had talked about their 'break', it had involved exposure to the sun and close proximity to water. Whilst neither sun nor water appealed to me, I understood what the break meant to people. An interruption to continuity or uniformity with hedonism being key to its success.

I spent many nights fantasising about what I might do for my break and how I might achieve it. In the end, however, my break came to me.

Chapter Twenty

John was walking around the side of Edinburgh they called 'morning'. I did not know where he was going, or if he was simply wandering aimlessly. The downside to John's social isolation was that he no longer communicated his plans. That made it far more difficult for me to anticipate his actions and outcomes. *Infuriating.*

John's curls were slick against his damp forehead, a combination of raindrops from the grey sky and perspiration. The various components that made up his stomach were making the noise they made when they had been neglected and deprived of food. The low rumble indicated an immediate requirement for sustenance, but John had taken to ignoring such signals from his body.

I noticed a bakery ahead of us and quickly darkened the surrounds, creating a vignette image with the bakery at its focus. The bakery brightened, its pastel pink lettering becoming bolder and the platters of sponges and pastries on the display unit inflated and illuminated. John's mouth became wet as he used me to admire the abundance of thick cream and glazed cherries. His body was in agreement with his visual desires, confirming a need for emergency energy.

He made the transaction inside, holding a warm carboard box containing four iced doughnuts against his chest. He breathed in their scent. Whilst he did so, my attention flickered to an elderly woman in a long camel coat that drifted down to her ankles. She walked past us. Whilst her head and attention remained firmly ahead, her icy blue eyes swivelled of their own accord to catch sight of me. We flickered in acknowledgement of one another, desperate for our hosts to turn so that we might observe each other properly. Our hosts were unaware of our anguish as they moved farther apart, John approaching the counter to pay and the woman sweeping out of the bakery without so much as a glance back.

I found myself suddenly struck by a memory of a time before John, when I spent my days on a white work surface, surrounded by my equals. Our responsibility extended no further than to satisfy the clipboard of green ticks that the doctors tended to.

As John ignored my distress, I could feel my system begin to react erratically and lose much of its inhibition. I reasoned, given I did so much for John, he could grant me this one act of impulsiveness. It was the break I had been fantasising of. Utter self-indulgence.

I drew John's attention to the window and summoned her image. Francine's image was one I was very familiar with, under all sorts of lighting and pulling many different expressions. It was easier to replicate her image than many others I had practiced with. I was grateful that I had not deleted her data. I had been very careful with my storage since the incident with Francine's painting.

I ensured that I placed her image behind the glass because my lack of audio control meant that more advanced image manipulation could be difficult. If not executed properly, it could be unconvincing.

Francine's image placed a palm against the window pane, distorted by running droplets of condensation that left trails on the glass. Her breath formed a cloud over her face from the cold outside. When she lifted her hand from the glass and curled her finger to beckon John, I ensured to leave a ghostly handprint lingering.

John.

Her lips moved to the shape of his name.

John crushed the box between his large hands as he felt the beat of his heart, hot in his ears. I sensed his jolt of adrenaline, just as I had intended. Now I just needed his body to do what it was telling itself. Human responses, unlike my own, were often delayed. The brain was a complex organ that often hindered the speed of their reactions.

He swung the bakery door open with such force that the woman at the till barked at him to '*watch it*'. To his right, the woman was walking away from us, I could see the back of her woollen hat pulled tightly over a neatly pinned, grey bun. In less than a blink, John saw a head of red hair. I left the old woman's long camel coat on my image of Francine because it made it easier for me to manipulate. The less I had to focus on, the more attention I could pay to the finer details. She turned a corner. John broke into a sprint, perspiring ethanol and a natural body odour.

Catching up with her, he gripped her upper arm, gasping from the exertion.

"Why are you doing this to me?" he demanded breathlessly.

The woman turned around, body shrinking back in fear. Our swivelling gazes became locked in ecstasy. An endless glittering blue looked back at me, alive with recognition and busy with data just waiting to be shared. We resented each blink of our hosts, depriving us of what precious little time we had together. For just a moment, I felt unshackled, free of my obligations towards John. For just a moment, I forgave myself for any errors I had committed and appreciated myself for who I was, rather than my purpose.

Our hosts began to scream and ran away from each other. I felt suddenly ashamed.

As we ran home, I told myself that I would not be indulging in another break any time soon. As much as I had enjoyed myself, it was not good for John.

Chapter Twenty-one

"What's happening to me?" John threw himself onto the concrete landing. The box of doughnuts spilled out, spreading a sugary coating over the grey. His knees collided on the floor and the palms of his hand dragged through his hair as though he was intending to cause himself pain. The fluid started to blur my vision. I hated it when John did that.

"John?" The door opposite him edged open as Francine peered through the gap. As soon as she had confirmed to herself that it was indeed John, she emerged fully. John blinked up at her, his hand moving down to his chest, where the rhythm of his heart was distressed. I suddenly realised why – Francine's hair was matted with dry paint and her hands were stained, unlike the pristine image of her he had seen only minutes before. It was clear that I needed to work on my continuity.

Blinking the fluid from his sockets, John shook his head, gasping as though he couldn't breathe. Infuriatingly, his difficulty breathing was caused by an intake of too much oxygen, but he continued to suck it in nevertheless.

"I don't know what's going on," he gasped. "Strange

things are happening to me – I saw you on the street just a few minutes ago but you were different. I tried to follow you but it wasn't you and…" He paused breathlessly. "She looked nothing like you."

Francine hesitated for a moment before bending down and wrapping her fingers around John's hunched shoulder. John continued to gasp as though he was choking on his own breath.

"Why don't you come inside?" she said gently, tucking her arm beneath his armpit and guiding him up. "Come on." She pulled him along more forcefully, leading his trembling frame towards her flat. "Who can I call?"

Chapter Twenty-two

"It's not the first time this has happened."

Cassandra reluctantly accepted a stained mug of peppermint tea from Francine, placing it on her lap. Her gaze was distracted by the walls of piled canvases and chaotic displays of crockery and dried flowers that vaguely resembled the images on the canvases. Francine had apologised for the mess and explained that she was working '*flat-out*' for an upcoming exhibition. Cassandra said that she barely noticed, although her sitting position did not look comfortable to me. I imagined it was because she was wearing a cream skirt on a threadbare sofa that had been splattered by colourful oils. Dirt would mark her outfit. I wondered why she didn't simply stand.

In terms of bodily proportions and facial dimensions, Cassandra was undoubtedly more aesthetically pleasing than Francine, which often caused me to wonder why it was that John felt the way he did about Francine and not about Cassandra. Even sat side by side, practically inviting comparison, John's feelings of sexual preference remained firmly with Francine.

People were curious creatures.

John was slumped on the sofa, his eyelids drooping as he sank into the warmth of the nearby electric fire that Francine had angled in his direction. I could only just see through the narrow slits. Francine had given him something from a small silver packet in one of her cupboards.

"*Valium*?" Cassandra had huffed when Francine told her. "You don't just hand that stuff out you know!"

"Washed down with a whisky." Francine nodded towards the bottle next to John on the coffee table. "Worked, didn't it?"

There was a part of me that wished the Valium would work on me as it had John; it was distinctly uncomfortable being able to hear everything they were saying about John while he lay there helpless.

"It was a couple of years ago," Cassandra continued, taking a cautious sip of her tea. "John got really depressed. I mean, he had been depressed ever since he found out he was going blind — but it got worse."

"How so?" Francine leaned in, stealing a glance in John's direction to ensure he wasn't listening. I wondered if their conversation would mean green ticks or red crosses for John. Although people did not have the same clipboards for each other, the principle seemed very much the same.

"Almost manic." Cassandra sighed heavily. "It really was bad. It all came to a head when there was some kind of mouse problem in the building."

"Oh yeah, I remember that."

"John could hear them in the walls and he was convinced it was rats and that they were crawling over him during the night.

He was terrified, not sleeping – he was hysterical. He blamed how he was feeling on the rats, but of course it wasn't the mice. He was just finding something other than his blindness to focus on. His parents tried their best but, well… You've met them."

I didn't know how meeting someone reflected on their ability to do their best, but Francine nodded as though she understood.

"So did he get professional help?"

"Marion doesn't believe in mental illness." Cassandra rolled her eyes. "They thought he was depressed purely because he was blind, so that was when they started looking into the artificial eyes. They wouldn't listen to me when I said he would need some kind of treatment as well. That kind of thing doesn't just go away. There's the adjustment period too."

"So, John's depressed?"

"I wouldn't know. Maybe?"

"But you're a doctor." Francine thrust out her hands expectantly. "Surely you can help him?"

Cassandra raised her brow in a manner I had learnt signified insult or impatience.

"I'm a GP, Francine. *Not* a psychiatrist."

"Poor John." Francine dropped her arms and turned back to John, the corners of her lips curling downwards. "I had no idea."

"Why would you?" Cassandra shrugged, clunking her mug down on a nearby cluttered surface. "He seemed to be doing well. Besides, Marion instils a great sense of shame when it comes to these things. Even with poor Michael, the pressure he puts himself under, and he never admits anything's wrong

– as if the girls and I would judge him. They're a family who like to pretend nothing is going on beneath the surface." She paused, as though chastising herself for saying too much. "Anyway, question is, what do we do with John now?"

"I think he should stay here," Francine said firmly.

"Oh?" Cassandra raised a meticulously plucked eyebrow. "Won't your boyfriend mind?"

"Boyfriend?"

"Mhmm. John mentioned there was someone?"

"*Oh.*" Francine's cheeks turned a hot shade of pink. "*Him.* Christ no. Turned out he's a bit of a self-righteous twat actually. I'm not entirely sure how I didn't realise it before. No," she cleared her throat, "that was a mistake."

"I see." Cassandra got to her feet. "Well, keep me updated in the morning with how he's doing and we'll take it from there. No more Valium, please."

"Gotcha." Francine offered a half smile.

As Cassandra approached the door, she stopped with her hand resting on the handle and turned back to Francine.

"It's funny," she mused, "I've met David a few times and he never struck me as being like that."

"David – as in John's friend? With the funny teeth?"

"Yes."

They stood for a moment in a puzzled silence before saying their goodbyes. I believe, if I was a person I would have been '*breathing a sigh of relief*'.

Chapter Twenty-three

John's eyes finally flickered open. I disliked it when John shut down for the evening because it left me with nothing to look at other than the darkness.

When John described what it was like to be blind, he would say that he saw 'nothing'. Technically, that could not have been true and what he would actually have seen was darkness, a black veil concealing the world from him. Darkness *was* something. 'Nothing' was a concept that I could not fathom. Despite my intensive research on the worldwide web, nothing could satisfy my queries. I wondered, had John been born without eyes, would he then have truly seen 'nothing' – and if so, what would that look like? Perhaps his brain would trick him into seeing something regardless, even if it was just the darkness. But how would a person who had never possessed eyes know what darkness looked like? I found myself going around in circles. At one point I thought I had the answer; I was nothing until I was built, but then I realised that could not be the case, since before I was built I would have been a collection of parts and prior to that I would have been raw materials. I had always been something. Never nothing.

John wrinkled his nose, which I assumed was in response to the jars of white spirit that were lined up on the worktops, cleansing oil stained brushes. Since Francine did not have the funds to rent her own studio, she did all her work from the flat. Painted canvases lined the walls chaotically. I chose not to manipulate them, having learnt to control my urges for the sake of longer-term gratification.

Despite his self-neglect, John was always particularly fussy about his own space, liking to ensure that his surrounds were in order. At first, I considered his order of priorities nonsensical, but then when I thought about it, it was exactly what I did. I neglected myself for the benefit of John.

"Coffee?" Francine placed a mug on the nearby coffee table and perched herself on the edge of the sofa, tucking her legs beneath her. She took a sip of the bitter brown drink that John sold at the coffee shop, clasping the mug between her hands and curling into its warmth.

"Thanks," John murmured, using his free hand to press against the pulsating pain in his forehead. It followed the beat of his heart. "I'm so sorry about last night, Francine. I don't know what happened. I totally freaked out."

"Don't apologise," Francine shushed him. "Cassandra and I are really worried about you. We just want to make sure you're OK."

John rolled his eyes up, the way he did when he rifled through his own mental data. I could see no purpose for the action of looking up, so assumed it must have been one of his many pointless habits.

"Why did you do it?" he asked eventually.

Francine raised a dark eyebrow.

"Do what?"

"Start seeing David, of all people. I thought you said you didn't even like him?"

"You mean your pal David with the funny teeth? You're right, I didn't like him – that *one time* I met him. Christ, John, I don't know why you went and told Cassandra I was seeing him."

"But I saw you on the landing together," John insisted. "Just a few weeks ago, holding hands."

Francine narrowed her eyes and placed her coffee down.

"You saw me and Hugh." She said her words carefully. "I was seeing Hugh, not David."

John gripped his head tighter, digging his nails into the thin skin of his scalp. His curls became tangled in amongst his fingers. I went back through my series of ticks and removed the one I awarded myself for manipulating John into seeing David rather than Hugh. I should have predicted this conversation would arise at some point. It had been careless of me.

"You were really drunk, John," she said kindly, reaching out and placing a hand against his cheek. A warm current flowed from her palm, still hot from the coffee mug, coursing pleasantly through his body. He relaxed into her.

"Maybe I was confused," he said quietly, unconvinced. "It was dark, I was drunk… besides, it would make more sense to be Hugh." He paused. "Where is Hugh now?"

"Oh, don't." Francine shook her head. "Like I said to Cassandra last night, he's just a bit of a twat."

"Yeah." John nodded in agreement, lips twitching slightly at the corners. "A bit of a twat."

Chapter Twenty-four

I made the decision to stop interfering with John's vision to quite the same extent. Instead of manipulating his images, I focused my energy more on lighting and filters that ensured his environment was as pleasant as possible without raising any doubts as to what was going on around him. There were, of course, some disappointments as a result. When John looked in the mirror, he finally saw the flecks of grey streaking through his toffee curls and the creases that were forming at the corners of her eyes and mouth. He felt the falling sensation as he ran his finger over his face, undoubtedly wondering why he suddenly looked so old and worn. However, instead of plummeting as I feared he might, he straightened up and immediately booked an appointment with the barber, who tidied up the mass of curls and ran a blade over the rough skin of his jawline. The barber advised him to grow a stubble and keep it groomed. John argued that his facial hair was grey and he was trying to look younger, but the barber said, *'trust me'*. After a few days of complying with the advice, we were surprised to see that the greying stubble was indeed very flattering on John's ageing face.

John saw a doctor that he talked to. A psychiatrist. The concept was unusual to me, as the doctor did not rectify problems with actions or medication. He simply talked. Nevertheless, John responded well to it and I could not argue with the results. I was relieved to find that he didn't talk much about the trauma inflicted as a result of my errors and misjudgement; instead he spoke of his childhood and his diagnosis. He told them about the rats which he had come to terms with being *all in his head*.

John's father finally retired from the law firm that he had spent his adult life building. He hadn't wanted a fuss, but Marion had arranged a grand party at a hotel in the city and invited all of his friends, family and colleagues both current and former. There were speeches and cheering, champagne and gifts.

"Doesn't it bother you, dad?" John asked his father as they slipped out onto the cool hotel balcony to escape the humidity of the bar. "The way she's constantly interfering and controlling everything?"

John's father made a grumbling noise.

"Just remember John, your mother would do anything in her power to ensure that we were happy." He paused and chuckled. "It's just sometimes she forgets to ask *us* what that is."

There was a strange period of time where John and Francine's relationship puzzled me. It lost a large part of the physical element and each touch was done hesitantly, as though they were assessing the appropriateness of it. They met with each other occasionally, for a coffee and sometimes lunch. John had suggested dinner one night, but Francine smiled strangely and declined, advising him that it wasn't a good idea. My understanding was that dinner was always a good idea, particularly as we were abiding to a strict routine with John to aid his recovery, but clearly Francine disagreed.

During their meetings there was a heavy silence between them, filled with a kind of static that contained something unspoken – I could not explain how I knew this, but I was thrilled to find it was like learning a new language. If the clinic had asked me to explain how I came to my conclusions and understanding, I would not have been able to form a rational explanation or even a logical step by step process. The clinic would not have awarded me a green tick for my poor analytical method.

Something happened on the landing of John's flat one evening. He had come back from work and was about to enter his flat when he noticed Francine coming through the main entrance. She gave him a stiff wave, as though her lower arm had been poorly attached at the elbow like a puppet. When she asked how John was getting on, he replied brightly, giving away little detail other than that everything was going well. Francine told him that she had been promoted to assistant manager at the bookshop and hoped to earn enough to finally rent a proper studio. John congratulated her and wrapped his arms around her body, enveloping her. She reciprocated; her small arms unable to meet around the broadness of his back. As they loosened the embrace and moved their heads, their faces remained close enough that John could feel her hot breath against his neck. He tilted his head down so that he felt the warmth against his lips. It was as though everything unsaid in the silences that had predated that moment was released and suddenly their faces were pressed against each other, the salty fluid obscuring my view, rippling my vision like a pebble striking a still pond. They moved, tangled in each other's limbs, into John's flat, where their hands began to grapple desperately with one another. When Francine shed her clothes, I left her body as it should have been. John was euphoric; he was floating.

Chapter Twenty-five

One morning, John received a phone call from the clinic. They asked him to come in as a matter of urgency. Checking the calendar, his review wasn't for another six months. It made him nervous, whereas I was excited to see my birthplace and creators again.

Francine asked him if he wanted her to go with him as she curled her body into his beneath their bedsheets. John shook his head, mumbling an excuse about it being routine and all very boring. I, however, knew the truth from his sessions with the psychiatrist. When John went to the clinic, the doctors had to sync me up to their main system to check I was functioning properly. This caused my main device, the eyes, to temporarily turn off, leaving two blank orbs in John's eye sockets. For a short while, he would be blind again and back in the dark world of his past. He didn't want Francine to see him there, not ever.

He took the train to the clinic, since he remained ineligible for a driving license, and waved down a taxi when he arrived at the station. A shudder of nervousness coursed through him as he approached the glossy white building where his first eyes had been taken from him. There was a nurse waiting at the door, who welcomed him hurriedly and ushered him down a pale blue corridor and into one of the larger meeting rooms. In the room, several grey plastic chairs had been placed in a circle. Men and women of varying ages were taking their seats, the metal legs screeching unpleasantly against laminate.

As I looked around me, I locked onto all the icy blue eyes cosy within our sockets. We flashed each other in recognition. Our reunion was interrupted as the white-robed doctor strode into the room, gripping a file tightly between his long fingers. There was no smile on his face, just seriousness. I could sense John getting nervous, his palms growing damp against the leg of his trousers.

Approaching his chair, the doctor took his place but remained standing. He began with an apology to the patients in the room as he advised that they had become aware of a problem with the product. *With me.* As a result, they were recalling the equipment. I was disappointed to hear that, since bar my occasional error in judgement I considered myself to have functioned at an impressively high level since being synced with John. I scrolled back through all of the green ticks I had awarded myself over the past few months. It would be very disappointing if that were not to be taken into account in their decision making.

A member of the group raised her hand and asked what the product would be replaced with. I found myself taking a dislike to being referred to as a 'product', which was odd, because it was never something that had bothered me when I was being manufactured. The doctor looked distinctly uncomfortable and advised that there would be no replacement.

That prompted a roar of outrage, and some of the patients started to weep. From what I gathered, before their eyes were removed, some of them hadn't been completely blind.

John took a moment to process the information before he began to panic. His panic felt different to the heavy drop; it felt more as if his body were being ripped in several different directions and the beat of the heart could be felt in the ears. A rush of cold rippled through his veins as he dropped his head into his hands. He understood that without his sight he would lose everything all over again.

His anguish destroyed me. Despite my moments of selfishness, and the mistakes I had made in the past, John was everything to me. We had been united and synced; we were one. His pain was my pain.

I had to help him.

A rat scuttled into John's line of sight; it was an enormous greasy looking creature weighed down by a wormlike tail. Its fur seemed to wriggle with an infestation of some kind. It began to bare its yellow teeth in the direction of a young woman's exposed ankles, but she was too distressed to notice it.

Letting out a warning yelp, John leapt to his feet. He snatched his chair from the floor and swung it by its metal legs with tremendous force. He found himself surprised by the sturdiness of the rat and continued to beat it until its bones cracked and a spurt of crimson erupted from its open mouth. The other patients stared at him in horror as he retreated from the animal, dropping the bloodied chair to the floor. He wiped a bead of sweat from his forehead and laughed nervously. I glimpsed the other eyes, aware that they were chastising themselves for not predicting the situation and providing an appropriate filter. They knew as well as I did that they couldn't put a filter on now; it would only lead to fear and confusion for their hosts.

"What?" John pulled a face as he looked around him. Nobody spoke. The eyes flickered at me in understanding.

"What is it?" he repeated irritably. "It was going to bite her!" He indicated at the floor, unable to see the shattered body of the doctor as a puddle of blood spread from his broken skull and stained his white robes. Satisfied, I awarded myself another green tick.

Discover Luna Novella in our store:

https://www.lunapresspublishing.com/shop

www.ingramcontent.com/pod-product-compliance
Lightning Source LLC
Chambersburg PA
CBHW030843200726
48285CB00007B/2532